P9-DDN-490

The Construction Crew

Lynn Meltzer

illustrated by
Carrie Eko-Burgess

Christy Ottaviano Books
Henry Holt and Company
New York

DANGER
HARD HAT
AREA

This old building's
Ready to fall
What do we need?
WRECKING BALL!

Dig now
Build later
What do we need?
EXCAVATOR!

Piles of earth
Push them over
What do we need?
BULLDOZER!

Move that boulder
Away we go
What do we need?
BACKHOE!

Tons of dirt
And lots of muck
What do we need?
DUMP TRUCK!

Pour the foundation—
That'll fix 'er
What do we need?
CEMENT MIXER!

Pound that nail
Drive that screw
What do we need?
CONSTRUCTION CREW!

Making holes
Sure takes skill
What do we need?
POWER DRILL!

The roof is high
Let's get there quicker
What do we need?
CHERRY PICKER!

We'll use our hands
If all else fails
What do we need?
**HAMMER AND
NAILS!**

"Make it flat,"
Says a stroller
What do we need?
STEAMROLLER!

Time to paint
Watch the spatter
What do we need?
EXTENSION
LADDER!

New home—
Good luck
What do we need?
MOVING TRUCK!

New friends
Swapping favors
What do we need?
CHEERFUL
NEIGHBORS!

On the wall
Let's hang a poem
What does it say?
HOME SWEET HOME!

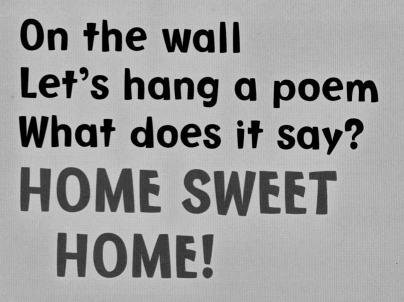

To Beth, who laid the foundation,
and to my family, who makes
our house a home
—L. M.

For my father, Charles Eko,
who told me when I was little
to quit tracing and start drawing
—C. E. B.

Henry Holt and Company, LLC
Publishers since 1866
175 Fifth Avenue
New York, New York 10010
www.HenryHoltKids.com

Henry Holt® is a registered trademark of Henry Holt and Company, LLC.
Text copyright © 2011 by Lynn Meltzer
Illustrations copyright © 2011 by Carrie Eko-Burgess
All rights reserved.

Library of Congress Cataloging-in-Publication Data
Meltzer, Lynn.
The construction crew / by Lynn Meltzer ; illustrated by Carrie Eko-Burgess. — 1st ed.
   p.   cm.
"Christy Ottaviano Books."
Summary: A construction crew tears down an old building and builds a new house in its place.
ISBN 978-0-8050-8884-7
[1. Stories in rhyme. 2. Construction equipment—Fiction. 3. Trucks—Fiction. 4. Building—Fiction.
5. Tools—Fiction.] I. Eko-Burgess, Carrie, ill. II. Title.
PZ8.3.M551553Co 2011   [E]—dc22   2010039763

First Edition—2011 / Designed by Véronique Lefèvre Sweet
The artist used Adobe Illustrator to create the illustrations for this book.

Printed in July 2011 in China by Toppan Leefung Printers Ltd., Dongguan City,
Guangdong Province, on acid-free paper. ∞

10 9 8 7 6 5 4 3 2 1

QUAKER STREET
NOV 1 2 2011